THE CHRISTMAS JUNK BOX

THE
CHRISTMAS
JUNK BOX

TONY KING

WOOD ENGRAVINGS BY MICHAEL McCURDY

David R. Godine, Publisher   Boston

I am grateful to Dawn Bursk who helped me greatly with
this manuscript and to Gregory Maguire who found her for me.

*

First edition published in 1987 by

David R. Godine, Publisher, Inc.
Horticultural Hall
300 Massachusetts Avenue
Boston, Massachusetts 02115

Library of Congress Cataloging-in-Publication Data

King, Tony
    The Christmas junk box.
    Summary: One Christmas Mr. Bones decides to give his
family a junk box, filled with odds and ends, instead of a shiny,
store-bought present.
    [1. Christmas—Fiction. 2. Gifts—Fiction]
I. McCurdy, Michael, ill. II. Title.
PZ7.K572Ch   1987   [E]   87-7386
ISBN 0-87923-694-9

First edition
Printed in the United States of America

Designed by Michael McCurdy

MR. Bones loves Christmas. It is his favorite time of year. He even whistles Christmas carols in summer, especially "The Holly and the Ivy." When people see him buying Christmas presents in February and March, he smiles and says, "Well, I guess Christmas is my hobby." But the part of Christmas Mr. Bones loves best is his family's own Christmas traditions.

On Christmas Eve, Mrs. Bones cooks a feast and puts candles on the table. Everyone gets dressed up. After dinner the family gathers around Mrs. Bones at the piano to sing Christmas carols. "Silent Night" is sung at least twice because it was playing when Mr. Bones asked Mrs. Bones to marry him. During the last carol, the children slip upstairs one by one, beginning with the youngest, to put on their pajamas. They climb up on their parents' big bed to hear Mrs. Bones read "The Night Before Christmas" from the same book her parents read to her when she was a child. After the Christmas stockings are hung over the fireplace, all four children bed down together in big sister's room.

Early Christmas morning the children climb back up on their parents' bed. "Merry Christmas! Merry Christmas! Merry Christmas!" they cry. There are plenty of Christmas hugs and kisses.

After the final treasure is removed from the toe of the last stocking, Mrs. Bones goes to the kitchen to make Christmas breakfast, and it is up to Mr. Bones to keep the children busy until it is ready. This is when, each year, he brings out his special gift for the whole family. It's always a surprise, and the children call it "the family present." Some past family presents were a wooden pony and cart big enough to ride in, a swing set with rings and a slide, a canoe, and an electric organ on which even the most unmusical Bones could thump out a satisfactory tune.

Then came the year of the Christmas Junk Box. Mr. Bones was tidying a closet that hadn't been touched in years when he found an old shoe box. MY JUNK BOX was written on the top. Inside he found worn and polished handles to a skip rope, some roller skate keys, and parts to his grandfather's fishing reel which he had taken apart long ago. Mr. Bones remembered a truck he had made out of odds and ends he found scattered around his parents' house. For headlights he used two brass buttons. His uncle had told him, "That is a fine vehicle, and you are a clever boy." It was at this moment that Mr. Bones decided to give his family a large junk box for Christmas. Mrs. Bones and the children could have fun making their own Christmas surprises.

Mr. Bones painted a sturdy wooden box red, blue, and green with white trim. He then searched his attic and basement for family treasures. And wherever he went for the next few weeks he kept his eye open for interesting odds and ends. He found a pair of old brass binoculars, two fold-out cameras, a toaster with sides you could wind down, colorful ribbons, silk squares,

pieces of lace, and mismatched knee socks for making puppets. He added wooden boxes of different sizes and tin boxes with pictures on top, some full of sea shells. There were spools and bobbins of various sizes, some with and some without thread. And, of course, lots of buttons including several brass buttons. He even found several old-fashioned alarm clocks.

By the morning of Christmas Eve, the red, blue, and green box with the white trim was chock-a-block full. And just before Mr. Bones closed the top for the last time, he filled the corners with string, glue, crayons, paint, and scissors.

That night, after the feast and the carols, and the stockings, and after all four children were bedded down in big sister's room and even Mrs. Bones was sleeping quietly, Mr. Bones put the junk box under the Christmas tree. And humming "The Holly and the Ivy" he went to bed.

On Christmas morning Mr. Bones woke up smiling. He could hardly wait for his children and Mrs. Bones to see the Christmas junk box. As he lay there in the dark thinking over all the past family presents, it suddenly occurred to him that every one of them had been store bought, wrapped in fancy paper, bright and shiny, and *new*. He wondered if his dear wife and sweet children deserved something better this Christmas morning than an old box full of junk, collected from dusty and forgotten corners. He wished his children would come soon or that Mrs. Bones would wake up. He needed some Christmas hugs and kisses.

While the children opened their stockings, Mr. Bones worried whether or not the junk box would be a success. As Mrs. Bones went to the kitchen, Mr. Bones led the children to the Christmas tree where the large box painted red, blue, and green with white trim sat waiting. He suggested they open it up while he got ready for breakfast.

When Mr. Bones came downstairs at last, the
children were laughing and smiling and handing
each other things, and Mrs. Bones, who had
come out of the kitchen to see what all the com-
motion was about, already had a handful of ribbons and was rummaging around in the junk

box for something else. She looked up at Mr. Bones and gave him a big smile. Together, two children were making the dashboard for the cockpit of a jet plane, using the dials from alarm clocks. Another had collected a little pile of magnets and springs and refused to tell Mr. Bones what she was making.

"You'll see," she said, "it's going to be a surprise."

The youngest boy was obviously making a truck, which he held up for his father to admire.

"Look, Dad, I'm making a truck!"

Mr. Bones said, "That's a fine vehicle, and you are a clever boy!"

"The only trouble is, I don't know what to make the headlights out of."

And Mr. Bones said, "Have you thought of trying brass buttons?"

Several years have passed since the year of the Christmas junk box, and Christmas at the Bones' is the same as ever. But everyone always agrees that the very best family present was the Christmas junk box.

This book was set in Linotype Palatino, a typeface
designed by Hermann Zapf. Named after Giovanbattista
Palatino, a Renaissance writing master, Palatino was
the first of Zapf's typefaces to be introduced to America.
The designs were made in 1948; the fonts for the
complete face were issued between 1950 and 1952.

* * *

This book was designed, illustrated, and typeset by
Michael McCurdy. Printed by Daamen, Inc., in Rutland,
Vermont, on Monadnock Natural, the book
was bound by Horowitz/Rae,
Fairfield, New Jersey.

* * *